HAUNTED REFLECTIONS

PART 2

Andrew J. Wilding

Copyright © 2021 by Andrew J. Wilding.

ISBN: Softcover   978-1-953537-44-7

Printed in the United States of America.

To order additional copies of this book, contact:
Martin and Bowman
1-855-921-1348
www.martinandbowman.com

IGGY AND WORMY

INTRO

The second part of this series takes place after Scarecrow has passed away-buried among with other great warriors in the mountains where the Merman lived. A new owner is needed for the "Flame of Creation". The Merman would not take the sword for themselves because they have too much pride and respect for both Scarecrow and the "Flame of Creation". The "Flame of Creation" itself, it is not just an ordinary sword-it is a "living" sword-alive that is. You see, the "Flame of Creation" has two souls-one is Jeremy Andrews A.K.A. Scarecrow and Queen Sandra. Scarecrow has a pure-hearted soul while Queen Sandra has an evil-hearted soul. The "Flame of Creation" can't have two souls in the sword because the sword was created just to have ONE soul, just like the village folk, creatures and the Merman-one soul for each living thing. So the "Flame of Creation" has to decide which soul to choose from. In order to do that is has to release both souls out of the sword and find new owners for these two souls OR create new owners. Which one will the "Flame of Creation"do? Create OR find two strangers worthy? Which ever the outcome is, it will go down in the history books of Hydra, just like Scarecrow did. But which soul OVERALL will be the best? Pure-hearted OR evil-hearted? Only time will tell.

CHAPTER 1

BURIAL OF KING SCARECROW

It was a sad day for everyone-the Merman, the people, the creatures and YES, even King Gobby (the creatures life span can live at least a thousand years or longer). The King of the Kingdom of Hydra is King Victor, descendant of the lines of Kings of King Luke, who was the very first King and King Josiah who was second at the thrown. King Victor is number nine in the family line of Kings. King Victor married a beautiful woman named Tina but she got killed in a climbing accident near where the Merman lived, that was another sad day as well. Plus, King Victor has NO children to take the place at the thrown as well. Could King Victor be the very last one at the thrown at the Kingdom of Hydra?

King Gobby written something on the headstone for King Scarecrow. It said, "The body my perish but the soul lives on". Everyone thought that was very nice of King Gobby (who engraved it on the headstone-personally). Everyone said prayers for Scarecrow then left, very sad and very upset (crying that is).

The "Flame of Creation" was not buried with King Scarecrow because it was nowhere to be found. Everyone thought that it was very strange because NO ONE never saw anyone leave with the sword at hand at King Scarecrows Keep.

King Gobby walked over to King Victor and said, "I think I know where the "Flame of Creation" is at, my friend". King Victor looked at him puzzled, then said, "It is nice to see you again Gobby. So where is the "Flame of Creation"? "To the very place where it all started, the very place Scarecrow became Scarecrow. The very place Scarecrow killed the fake Scarecrow (who was Queen Sandra at that time). King Victor grinned at King Gobby and said, "At the waterfall, near the farm plains of Eternal? Makes perfect sense if you ask me". "Exactly" said King Gobby.

"We should head over there AFTER everything is finished up here", said King Victor. "I agree", said King Gobby, both looking at each other with worry and concern on both of their faces. "But we should go over there, just the BOTH of us and find out what the "Flame of Creation" is up to and WHY the sword is at the waterfall as well, my friend", said King Victor. "I just hope and pray it is nothing too bad OR too serious because I really don't want to see another war break out", said King Gobby. King Victor answered back, "I agree with you, one hundred percent. That was so war battle, five hundred years ago, according to the records". "It was indeed, I know, I was THERE and I really don't want to fight in a battle like that one again", said King Gobby, thinking even harder then ever.

CHAPTER 2

THE "FLAME OF CREATION"

Meanwhile, at the waterfall, the very place where Jeremy Andrews became Scarecrow, there it is, the "Flame of Creation" (Gobby was right about the whereabouts of the sword). But something was different about the "Flame of Creation". It was glowing TWO different sides of colors-one is half blue (which is the symbol of Scarecrow) and the second one is mixed with red, black and grey (which is the symbol of Queen Sandra).

The blue light of the sword left and the other half of the light, which is red, black and grey, left the sword as well. The "Flame of Creation" then turn ash and vanished into thin air. The two separate balls of light turned into TWO creatures-one is blue and the other is mixed with red, black and grey. This would be the turning point for the future of all living things and the country of Hydra FOREVER.

CHAPTER 3

IGGY AND WORMY ARE BORN

The ball of blue light transformed into a very, small creature-eyes were yellow-about 4 foot 8-long, thin, white hair-sharp teeth-pointy ears-long nails on both hands and feet and his clothing is brown and green and named himself, Iggy. The second ball of light, red-black and grey, transformed into a very heavy build and tall creature-the same features as Iggy but his height is 6 foot 4 and the creature named himself Wormy. How they knew their names is because when they were born, there first words their names-Iggy and Wormy. The next thing they both did is look at each other, almost like a stare-down, for the longest time. Finally, Wormy spoke first, "So, you are here in front of me to see if you are capable of handling the powers of the "Flame of Creation", right"? "Funny", answered Iggy, "I was thinking the same thing". Wormy grinned and later said, "My name is Wormy". Iggy smiled, "And my name is Iggy". They both shake hands and step back quickly. "The "Flame of Creation" told me", "Only ONE of us will be the guardian of the power", "but I thought TWO of us would be the guardians of the power". Iggy answered back in a angry tone, "The "Flame of Creation" told me the same thing".

Wormy answered back, in a dragon-like laugh, "I guess there are TWO choices, IGGY". "And what is that, WORMY"?, said Iggy, in a snappy tone in his voice. "HA, HA, HA", laughed Wormy, "Either you and myself work together OR we fight it out, the old-school way, YOU-AND-ME". Iggy glared back at Wormy. Iggy replied back and said, "The "Flame of Creation" told me we are expecting visitors soon so how about WE ask them and then decide if we go "old-school" or not-DEAL"? Wormy grin back at Iggy and said, "I love it when two individuals think OR have the same mind. OK, DEAL". They both shock hands again and waited for King Gobby and King Victor to arrive.

CHAPTER 4

JOURNEY TO THE WATERFALL

After, everyone went home after the burial of King Scarecrow, King Gobby ask one of the creatures to get permission to ride one of the Gob-wings. As the years passed, some of the creatures evolve into bigger forms, a lot of them did, like growing wings. They are Goblins with wings (almost like giants). Riding a Gob-wing would take about ten hours to reach the waterfall entrance (it is a lot better on foot because that way it would take about a week). King Gobby and King Victor got permission to ride ONE of the Gob-wings because these creatures are very picky who gets to ride on them. Gob-wings would give a ride to any King OR Queen, without permission (sometimes, depending on their mood). Anyone else would have to pay for their services like give them food and drink, a lot of it.

And off they went to the waterfall. While riding the Gob-wing, King Gobby said to King Victor, "I see a lot of beauty at this height and I hope it remains like this. " I hope so", said King Victor, with concern on his face. After a while, King Gobby looked over at King Victor and said, "I believe someone OR SOMETHING is waiting for us at the waterfall". "I thought it was me Gobby but I have the same feeling likewise", said King Victor. It took no-time at all for the Gob-wing to arrive at the waterfall entrance. King Gobby ask the Gob-wing to wait for them. And off they went, King Gobby and King Victor to enter the entrance of the waterfall.

CHAPTER 5

ENCOUNTERING IGGY AND WORMY

When King Gobby and King Victor enter the waterfall area, there waited patiently, Iggy and Wormy. "What took you so long", said Iggy, with a greasy grin on his face. King Gobby and King Victor looked at each other surprised. After for a while, King Victor said to both Iggy and Wormy, "You both were expecting us"? Wormy grinned at both King Gobby and King Victor, later said, "The "Flame of Creation" told both of us that we are going to see someone and my guess is that it is you two, YES"? And again King Gobby and King Victor looked at each other again, surprised. Then, King Gobby answered back at both Iggy and Wormy, "Pardon my manners, my name is King Gobby, from the Kingdom of Hope, King of the creatures and this man standing right next to me is King Victor of the townspeople at the Kingdom of Hydra." Iggy and Wormy looked at each other for a bit and Iggy said afterwards, "My name is Iggy and this other creature here is name Wormy. WE both came out of the "Flame of Creation". "Very interesting", said King Gobby, "You must represent King Scarecrow because of your skin color and Wormy here represents Queen Sandra by your skin color, makes sense." King Gobby added, "I said to Victor here, at first, the "Flame of Creation" must have went to this very location and I was right. Also, I said to Victor that there MIGHT be someone OR something waiting for us when we enter the entrance of the waterfall as well. Does that answer your question, Wormy"? Wormy glared at King Gobby, shock his head at him and said, "YES".

Iggy walked a little closer to King Gobby and King Victor, then said to both of them, "Who is KING SCARECROW and QUEEN SANDRA"? "Scarecrow is a dear friend of myself and King Victor here, said King Gobby. "King Scarecrow's color is blue, pure-hearted, while Queen Sandra's color is red, black and grey, evil-hearted". King Victor jumped in and ask a quick question to both Iggy and Wormy, "I have a question for both of you, why would the "Flame of Creation" separate itself to form two creatures such as yourselves"? "Good question", added King Gobby.

Wormy walked over to get some water at the waterfall, turn around and said, "The "Flame of Creation" cannot have two souls into the sword itself so the "Flame of Creation" separate itself into two forms-myself and Iggy". Wormy looked over at Iggy, took a deep breathe and said, "Now myself and Iggy here must decide here which route to choose from. Either both of us fight it out, one-on-one to see whoever gets the power of the "Flame of Creation" OR we both work together to handle the power".

Iggy said right after Wormy, "By working together is by fusing both souls into one, myself and Wormy, You see, GOBBY and VICTOR, you both know KING SCARECROW and QUEEN SANDRA very well, right? How about this, you both help myself and Wormy here to decide which path to take, DEAL"? Wormy looked over at Iggy and grinned, mean-looking wise. "DEAL", said King Victor. "Me as well", said King Gobby.

CHAPTER 6

KING GOBBY TELLS THE STORY ABOUT KING SCARECROW AND QUEEN SANDRA

King Gobby and King Victor walked over to Iggy and Wormy, sat down next to both of them. King Gobby later said to both Iggy and Wormy, "I will do the talking, both of you will listen to me, pay attention to every detail to what I have to say, but remember, myself and King Victor here are HELPING you both, nothing more-nothing less, OK"? Iggy and Wormy both grinned at King Gobby, then at each other (horrible, mean-looking grins). Soon after, Wormy said, "OK, BOSS, HA, HA, HA". Iggy laughed as well (and again, horrible laughs they were, just like the fake Scarecrow, along with his minions-the Grave Diggers). King Victor leaned over to King Gobby and whisper to him in his ear, "DE-JA-VIEW". King Gobby looked over at King Victor and raised his eyebrows.

"OK", said King Gobby, "I will tell you both each who King Scarecrow and Queen Sandra is. King Scarecrow is not his REAL name. His real name is Jeremy Andrews. The creatures in the afterlife brought him here with their power, five-hundred years from the future, with the help from my brother Hope. They needed King Scarecrow to make weapons for us creatures to raise up against King Luke and his men. You see, King Scarecrow has a gift to make a lot of different powerful, light weapons, of any kind you can think of. In the past, Hope betrayed me because of my popularity with the other creatures and in return Hope ask the other creatures help to change the fate of all of us"

Gobby took a deep breathe and added, "The rest of the creatures agree with Hope, including myself. So I sent King Josiah, who is my best friend and passed away-God bless him, to go get King Scarecrow and bring him here. I gave

King Josiah a one-shoot deal into transforming a human being into a creature. So King Josiah transformed Jeremy Andrews into King Scarecrow, which in fact look like a scarecrow, out in the farm fields. But the plan was back-fired by Queen Sandra, she hated the creatures that much, she trick them ALL, including myself and King Josiah into being friends and making peace. She even made King Luke jealous of herself and me because he thought and even HEARD from someone, from my brother Hope, that we both had an affair, which was not true at all what-so-ever".

"So King Scarecrow was given the 'Flame of Creation" by my brother Hope, at the Kingdom of Hope, at that time it was abandon. But the sword was tamper by Queen Sandra and made King Scarecrow evil-even took control over his body. Queen Sandra learned ALL of this in the afterlife, about what Hope was doing and planning. Queen Sandra created a new breed of half-human and half-creatures called Grave Diggers with the "Flame of Creation", which look like King Scarecrow. Queen Sandra created ten-thousand strong-at-least Grave Diggers and marched right up at the gates of the Kingdom of Hydra. We fought hard and won the battle, with the help on the Mermen but it wasn't over right there. The fake Scarecrow, who is Queen Sandra, confronted the REAL Scarecrow, who became King of the Mermen. King Scarecrow picked up the "Flame of Creation" drove it through the body, killing him".

"Soon after, Queen Sandra appeared in front of King Scarecrow and told him that it was all her fault and all her doing. King Scarecrow forgave Queen Sandra and after King Scarecrow went back to his time, with the help of Queen Sandra, five-hundred years in the future. After, myself and King Josiah heard about this story from Queen Sandra, and soon decided to give King Scarecrow a gift by making him King of the Mermen, along with the "Flame of Creation" to his name." Gobby looked over at King Victor and then back at Iggy and Wormy, "Myself and King Victor just came from King Scarecrows funeral, buried him, died of old age or should I say, his guilt of what he did to the creatures, people and even the Mermen. Even though King Scarecrows body was being controlled by Queen Sandra, he still killed off a lot of them".

"That concludes my story up until now, Iggy and Wormy. Do you both have any questions for myself and King Victor? Maybe my story can help you decide which side to take. I really, really think you both don't want to be in any part in any war. No violence, no killing. I think peace would be the best choice, I think so". "I agree", said King Victor, nodding his head up and down. Iggy and Wormy just stared at King Gobby and then back at each other, didn't know what to make out of the story King Gobby has told both of them. After, Iggy looked right at King Gobby and said, "I think, I and WORMY made up our minds of which side to take". "EXACTLY", said Wormy.

CHAPTER 7

IGGY'S AND WORMY'S DECISION

King Gobby looked over at King Victor and later back at both Iggy and Wormy, with greasy grins on both of their faces. "So, what is your decision? Peace? OR War"?

Iggy got up, walked over a little towards King Gobby and King Victor, then said, "Myself and Wormy's decision is WAR". "Peace is for the women, HA, HA, HA", added Wormy. "WHAT", shouted King Victor. Gobby got up and said, "May I ask WHY you both have chosen war and not make peace with us creatures, Mermen and human beings? WE haven't wrong you so WHY"? "YES, tell us WHY", there has to be a reason for this. Myself and Gobby would like a clear-head on this issue", said King Victor, red in the face.

Wormy walked a bit closer towards King Gobby and King Victor, looked over at Iggy, laughed a bit and said, "That's easy. So you can have your friend back with you, KING SCARECROW that is, HA, HA, HA. You should be happy with yourselves". " Myself and Wormy can bring back your friend, King Scarecrow, back from the dead". King Gobby and King Victor just stared at Iggy and Wormy of what they have both said. In total, complete shock, eyes wide-opened, didn't know what to make out of it.

CHAPTER 8

IGGY'S AND WORMY'S SURPRISE

"How can you do that, bring back King Scarecrow from the dead"? said King Gobby, very concern for the very moment. "I think it is time for myself, Iggy, to tell you our side of the story, OK"? "Myself and Gobby are all ears, said King Victor. "That's FANTASTIC", said Wormy, along that silly grin on his face as usual.

Iggy went to the waterfall (just like Wormy did) to get a drink of water and began to tell his side of the story. "Where shall I and Wormy begin"? said Iggy. "You go first", said Wormy. "Fine, I will go first then", said Iggy. Iggy took a deep breathe then winked at King Gobby (because Gobby have done that when he told his side of the story) and started.

"I will begin with the "Flame of Creation'. The sword told both of us there is some benefits with the power or should I say already put that knowledge in both of our heads, myself and Wormy. The benefits is that if we fuse together, the King of the creatures and the King of the people can bring back ONE person OR creature from the dead-alive that is but there is a draw-back on that and if you would so kindly tell the rest of the story Wormy, if you please, ha, ha, ha," "With pleasure", smiled Wormy. "The draw-back is that WE have to fight your kind to see who gets ownership of the "Flame of Creation" and rule this country of Hydra and this Planet".

"I know King Scarecrow much better then both of you and I tell you now King Scarecrow would not want another to break out", said King Gobby. King Victor nodded his head up and down.

"I already know that BUT this is what, myself and Wormy wants at the end of the day",said Wormy, very serious looking this time. "But there is also another gift that whoever you bring back, he or she or WHATEVER can use a one-shot-deal with summoning a powerful creature to aid you. In return, WE, Iggy and Wormy, can create soldiers, just like King Scarecrow OR Queen Sandra, which ever you want to put it, ha, ha, ha", added Iggy. "And how many creatures OR soldiers can you make. The "Flame of Creation" must have told you that as well", King Victor said to Iggy. "About half a million soldiers. How many can you get, ha, ha, ha", laughed Iggy. King Victor looked over at King Gobby, then back at Iggy and Wormy and said with a smile on his face, "About the same BUT my soldiers and the creatures have experience, your minions have NONE". "How do you like those apples now", smiled Gobby.

Iggy and Wormy just stared at King Gobby and King Victor and later back at each other-no smiling-no laugher-NO NOTHING.

CHAPTER 9

DRAWING THE LINE

"You are not laughing, I am insulted", smiled King Victor, as he looked over at King Gobby. "Do you still want to go to war"?, asked King Gobby. Iggy and Wormy looked at each other again and later back at King Gobby and King Victor. Wormy stood up, full of anger and answered King Gobby in full rage, "YES, I STILL WANT TO GO TO WAR, ALONGSIDE WITH IGGY".

King Victor stood up and returned the favor back at Wormy, "IF YOU WANT A WAR, WE WILL GIVE YOU A WAR. WE WILL HIT YOU HARD AND MAKE YOU RUN, LIKE MICE".

Soon after Iggy got up and shouted back, "WE WILL SEE IF THAT VISION OF YOURS COMES TRUE THEN". Iggy took a deep breathe and shouted again, "MYSELF AND WORMY WILL MAKE AN ARMY THAT THE SO-CALLED KING HERE GOBBY WITNESSED BEFORE. WE WILL BRING BACK THE GRAVE DIGGERS BACK TO LIFE. SO, WHAT DO YOU THINK OF THOSE APPLES, GOBBY"?

Wormy said afterwards, as he calm down a little, "This will be our base. When we fuse together, we will have a different name, how about IGWORM"? "I like it A LOT", smiled Iggy.

"We shall take our leave, come on Victor, lets go",said King Gobby, looking very worried and scared at the same time. "Fine", said King Victor, still angry. As when King Gobby and King Victor exited the waterfall entrance and ready themselves on the Gob-wing, who is patiently waiting for them all this time, Iggy and Wormy came out soon after, watching. Wormy said to both King Gobby and King Victor, "The next time we meet, it will be in the battlefield". King Victor answered back, before the Gob-wing left, "And WE will be waiting for you".

CHAPTER 10

BREAKING NEWS

It took no-time for the Gob-wing to make it back to the Kingdom of Hydra. King Gobby and King Victor landed in the towns square (which is the center of the town, inside the castle gates). Everyone gathered around to greet both Kings but they all saw something on the Kings faces, something very wrong indeed.

King Gobby went to one of the creatures and said to him, "I want you and a few others to bring me the village leader from Lost Woods, at the village called Cherry Blossom and also bring the tribal leader, who now settles in between the swamps and the mountains, up north is where he is. Ride the Gob-wing, getting permission should not be an issue. They are a lot faster then traveling on by foot. Now go, QUICKLY". So the little creature did want King Gobby asked, without question and off they went on the Gob-wing.

King Victor said afterwards, "We have breaking news to tell you all. I know we have buried King Scarecrow, God bless him, a very sad moment for us all but we might be facing war very soon, a lot sooner then you all think". King Victor asked everyone to gather around and listen to what he and King Gobby has to say to everyone.

It took a good hour to tell this horrific story to everyone, both King Victor and King Gobby took turns telling the story. At the end of it all, everyone was in complete silence, not even a pin-drop to make a noise.

NEW INTRO

There will be two different parts, broken into two different events of this story. One is Iggy and Wormy-behind the scenes and the second part in King Gobby and King Victor-behind the scenes. When the time comes they will both meet AGAIN at the gates of the Kingdom of Hydra, which another war will go down into the history books of Hydra. Will King Scarecrow come back to life to fight? Will the Grave Diggers come back to life fight as well? Is this a trick that Iggy and Wormy is planning? Only time will tell.

CHAPTER 11

IGGY AND WORMY-DECIDING

"Can we both really bring back the Grave Diggers"? said Iggy. "I think we can because that information is stored in the power of the "Flame of Creation", right"?said Wormy. Iggy looked at Wormy and said, "But HOW can we do it, there is NO "Flame of Creation" in front of us". Wormy took a deep breathe and answered back at Iggy, "This is just a guess but I think the only way to bring the "Flame of Creation" back to life is to sacrifice ONE of us".

Iggy just stared at what Wormy have just said to him. After, Iggy said, "It makes sense if you look at it that way but who should we sacrifice then"? "Well", said Wormy, "If I sacrifice you, I can bring the Grave Diggers because I represent Queen Sandra-the evil-hearted side". "And if I sacrifice you, Wormy, I can create a new breed of creatures, right"? replied Iggy, with a lot of concern showing on his face.

Wormy got up, started to walk around a bit, turn around to look at Iggy and answered him, with a sad look on his face, "Yes, you are right but.......". "But what"? said Iggy. "I think I just figure it out how to bring the "Flame of Creation" back to life and at the end of the day, ONE of us must DIE. If we fuse together, like sacrifice both of ourselves, we can BOTH create an elite army of Grave Diggers or WHATEVER. If we fuse together like that Iggy, we can both LIVE, like two souls into ONE", said Wormy, showing a bit of relief his face and the same thing on Iggy's face as well.

"We should do that then", said Iggy. Wormy answered back quickly, "YES, I agree with this decision-one hundred percent". "We should get ready to make the sacrifice then", said Iggy. "But how do we do this, we have NO weapon of any kind to do this sacrifice", replied Wormy. Iggy turned around to look at Wormy and said, "We can both use our hands. We both have very sharp fingers". "True, so true", said Wormy.

After, both Iggy and Wormy stood in front of each other, ready their hands and then attack each other quickly, with their razor-sharp fingers, slicing each others throats. They both fell down on the ground, bled-out and died. Soon after, the bodies of Iggy and Wormy-DISAPPEAR, into thin air. After, the souls of Iggy and Wormy appeared and we into each other and form another body, a much larger, heavier one. The creature took his time to stand up and after he said, "IGWORM IS BORN, HA, HA, HA."

CHAPTER 12

KING GOBBY AND KING VICTOR-
BACK TO SQUARE ONE

"Here we go again, another war at the doorsteps, at the gates of the Kingdom of Hydra-OH JOY", said King Gobby, looking very sad and depressed. King Victor walked over to King Gobby, pat him on the shoulder and said, "The village leader and the tribal will be here soon. If it is a fight Iggy and Wormy wants, we will give both of them a good-going of a fight. We have more creatures, more people and YES, more Mermen to fight on our side, a lot more. More soldiers then five-hundred years ago. Would you like a cup tea, Gobby"?

King Gobby smiled at King Victor and said, "Yes, please".

Soon after a creature and two of King Victor's guard soldiers came rushing in the throne room. King Victor said to all three of them, "Any news"? "Yes, my Lord", said the creature, "The village leader and the tribal leader have arrived PLUS the head of the Mermen is here as well". "Good, sent all three of them to the thrown room as soon as possible", said King Victor. "Right away, my Lord," said the creature.

King Victor said with a smile on his face, "I think you and I need some exercise, to teach Iggy and Wormy a thing or two, like helping them both what the true meaning of life is all about, don't you agree"? King Gobby laughed and said, "You couldn't put it any better, ha, ha".

Later, the village leader, the tribal leader and the head of the Mermen entered the throne room. "Come in, sit down and have some tea, my friends. Myself and Gobby will tell you the situation of what is going on", said King Victor.

CHAPTER 13

IGGY AND WORMY A.K.A. IGWORM- NEW WEAPON

When Igworm got up from the ground, he looked like Wormy in height but also looked like Iggy in skin-color. The facial features are the same and the skin-color is mixed with red, black, grey and blue but overall more blue then the rest of the colors. Igworm looked at himself, saw his reflection into the water and laughed right out loud, "IT WORKED, WE HAVE FUSE TOGETHER AND IT FEELS GREAT, HA, HA, HA. "Now, where is the "Flame of Creation"? Are you hiding from me? Where are you"?

Afterwards, Igworms body glowed a deep, bright purple. There it is, right in front of Igworm, a brand-new "Flame of Creation", in a deep purple glow which looked more powerful then the old one. Igworm laughed and just of a sudden the "Flame of Creation" spoke to Igworm. Igworm silence his laugher. The "Flame of Creation"said, "When you make your new species of creations, you are not permitted to make any Grave Diggers because only the original owner can make them, not you". "Where is the fun in that", said Igworm, laughing in a low tone. "You are to make your species look like Iggy and Wormy ONLY and I will help you. Second, you can make a maximum of half a million of your new species, which you already know. Lastly and finally, I will give you a special gift, it is called the Warrior Job List".

Igworm said, "What is the Warrior Job List"? "I will tell you later but first let me help you make your new kind of species, your new Iggy's and Wormy's, OK"? said the "Flame of Creation". "You're the boss", grinned Igworm.

CHAPTER 14

KING GOBBY AND KING VICTOR-
PLANNING AHEAD

"Myself and Gobby would not ask you three to come here in short notice, after all this is a sad time for all of us. I know this is the burial day for King Scarecrow, so I will get right down to the point then", said King Victor.

King victor told the village leader, the tribal leader, and the head of the Mermen the entire story about the disappearance of the "Flame of Creation"up until leaving the waterfall entrance (which is where Jeremy Andrews became Scarecrow).

When King Victor finished telling the story, along side King Gobby, telling his side of the story, the village leader, the tribal leader and the head of the Mermen did not know what to make out of it all. "This is going to be worse than fighting King Scarecrow and his breed of Grave Diggers-five-hundred years ago to be exact. And WE might fight his minions AGAIN too", said the village leader. Everyone nodded their heads up and down.

The head of the Mermen stood up and said, "We must act NOW, plan ahead, get an early start before Iggy and Wormy does". "You are right", said the tribal leader. After, King Victor stood up and said, "I will get my people to make weapons, bows-n-arrows and swords and I ask you to do the same, please". Everyone nodded their heads "yes" to what King Victor have said just then.

"We will all make traps, like the ones in the past, have archers on the hilltops and on the mountain low range and even the castle front ends as well", said King Victor. After, King Gobby stood up and said, "There is no time to waste, lets tell EVERYONE and get started right away".

CHAPTER 15

IGWORM-IGGY AND WORMY MINIONS

"OK", said the "Flame of Creation", "First, we have to get a lot of fine sand because your new species must be made out of sand and water. As you can see we have LOTS of water, we just need some sand and there is should be some outside. Pick up these two empty water buckets and fill them up with sand, please" (these empty water buckets were the buckets Scarecrow left when he decide to leave to be the King of the Mermen).

So Igworm did what the "Flame of Creation" ask him to do. He got two buckets full of sand and headed on in back to where the "Flame of

Creation"was, by the waterfall. "Now, dump the sand right in the middle of the waterfall and after put myself, the "Flame of Creation"right in the middle, in the pile of sand which is now like soft mud, said the "Flame of Creation".

So Igworm did what he was told to do by the "Flame of Creation". Igworm waited and soon after all Igworm saw was the entire body of water turn different colors. "In the past", said the "Flame of Creation", "you were supposed to drive the sword into yourself to collect half of your soul to go into the "Flame of Creation" but since the sword already has a soul, two souls to be exact, you didn't need to do that now. Your new army of Iggy's and Wormy's will be at the gates of the Kingdom of Hydra. They will come out of the ground when you arrive there. Because there is no room for ALL of them here, understand"? "Like I said before "Flame of Creation", you are the boss", said Igworm, grinning and laughing in a low-tone.

CHAPTER 16

KING GOBBY AND KING VICTOR-
WARNING FROM THE HEAD OF THE MERMEN

Five hours later..... the head of the Mermen requested to speak to King Gobby, King Victor, the village leader and the tribal leader, in private in the throne room. After everyone settled in the throne room, the head of the Mermen stood up and said, "I have something to tell you and it is not good news".

King Gobby, King Victor, the village leader and the tribal leader all looked at each other, puzzled. "I know we are ALL busy getting ready to go to war AGAIN but I fear a much stronger force is among us Mermen might harm us badly....even ALL OF US. WE, Mermen, sense that feeling might be a giant or SOMETHING is going to attack us",said the head of the Mermen. "OR it might be the other way around", added King Gobby, raising his eyebrows. "I hope you are right King Gobby but I have a bad feeling about this, either GOOD OR BAD", said the head of the Mermen.

The head of the Mermen also added, "I also think strongly that the enemy is outside, at the city gates, right now, as I am telling you all this. I am not stupid BUT maybe its me and the rest of the Mermen thinking this, I don't know". "You are not stupid, you and the rest of the Mermen are very brave, powerful and WISE warriors. Whatever feeling you have, I am with you",said King Victor, as everyone nodded their heads up and down.

"We will keep this conversation to ourselves and work at the task ahead of us all. If we tell everyone about what the head of the Mermen told us might make everyone even more scared, OK"?, said King Victor, as everyone agree to keep this quit.

CHAPTER 17

IGWORM-WEAPON MAKING

"I have made two hundred and fifty thousand Iggy's and Wormy's each, a grand total of five hundred thousand, altogether. You will be very pleased, Igworm", said the "Flame of Creation". "It is already putting tears to my eyes", laughed Igworm.

"Now we will make you all kinds of different weapons like swords, shields, spears, tridents, bows-n-arrows, knives, staffs, sharp stars, strong armor and helmets, powerful magic and potions and the strongest hand-weapon of them all-the KATANA. But before I do that I need you, Igworm, to do the same thing just before. Go get the two water buckets, fill them up with sand and put it right in the middle of the waterfall, you are going to be pleased", said the "Flame of Creation", So Igworm did the same process again by getting two water buckets of sand from outside the entrance and dumping it right in the middle of the waterfall. Then Igworm again put the "Flame of Creation" right in the muddy pile of sand and watch the entire lake turn different colors, like a rainbow.

"I have a question for you, how do you know so much by making ALL these weapons"? said Igworm. The "Flame of Creation" answered, "Time will tell, my friend Igworm, but for now let me concentrate on making these fine weapons, OK"? "You're the boss, said Igworm, not laughing low this time, just a lot of question marks all over head instead.

CHAPTER 18

KING GOBBY AND KING VICTOR-GOB-WINGS

As everyone started working on making weapons, setting up traps, gathering rocks, etc. Everyone took taking turns in helping because everyone needed breaks-even the Gob-wings helped out in making weapons, setting up traps, gathering rocks, and EVEN cooking food for everyone. No one expected TWO things to happen on the same day. One is doing all this work on the burial day of King Scarecrow and second is the Gob-wings helping out because they are very stuck-up and only help themselves mostly (according to their past).

But when war is at the door-step between GOOD verses EVIL, the Gob-wings would thought this would be a good opportunity to show everyone what they are really made out of. King Gobby, King Victor, the village leader, the tribal leader and the head of the Mermen were very impressed and pleased with the Gob-wings (and they didn't even ask permission from the Gob-wing to help out, they just went on and did it).

One of the Gob-wings said to King Gobby that the creatures, the people and the Mermen can ride them into battle. They only want one thing in return-to be remembered all through history of what they have done for everyone. King Gobby, King Victor, the village leader, the tribal leader and the head of the Mermen agreed with this proposal, without question.

CHAPTER 19

IGWORM-WARRIOR JOB LIST

"Only time will tell", Igworm said to himself, repeatedly. That is what the "Flame of Creation" said to Igworm about making ALL of these weapons.

"As I mentioned to you earlier Igworm", said the "Flame of Creation", about the Warrior Job List". "Yes, what is this WARRIOR JOB LIST"?, said Igworm. "I will tell you ALL of the information to you, OK"? said the "Flame of Creation". "I want you to listen very carefully and listen to me well because you have to choose half of them and not ALL of them", added the" Flame of Creation".

Soon after, the "Flame of Creation" started to spin very slowly until it reach a certain speed. The "Flame of Creation" quickly shot a purple beam of light and enter Igworms head, it was the entire Warrior Job List.

Here is the list the "Flame of Creation" has put into Igworm's head. At the end of it, Igworm has to choose half of them for his new army, his new species, his new Iggy's and Wormy's.

WARRIOR JOB LIST

1. <u>SQUIRE:</u> Training day and night to become good fighters, they aren't too useful in the beginning. But remember, everything takes time.

2. <u>CHEMIST:</u> Attacks with a wide knowledge of various items. A very valuable party member, especially for back-up.

3. <u>ARCHER:</u> With super-creature eyesight, they use bows against long-distance enemies.

4. <u>KNIGHT:</u> Physically and spiritually strong, they learn powerful new techniques by mastering sword skills.

5. <u>MONK:</u> Martial-art experts who have disciplined their minds and bodies for years. Their fists are more deadly then weapons.

6. <u>BLACK MAGE:</u> Create thunder and flame from the spirit, using powerful magic not to destroy but to protect allies.

7. <u>WHITE MAGE:</u> Best at healing aiding allies in battle. They fight to protect the weak and deflect the forces of darkness.

8. <u>TIME MAGE:</u> Use time magic to control time and space. Extremely useful allies.

9. <u>SUMMONER:</u> Summon powerful monsters from the other side making them fight for you.

10. <u>THIEF:</u> With agile bodies and quick hands. They use various stealing techniques to confuse enemies.

11. <u>GEOMANCER:</u> All objects under heaven and earth are their weapons and they make full advantage of it as well.

12. <u>LANCER:</u> Heavy armor flying dragons, these knights created a unique way

to fighting. Skilled with spears, jump attacks and defense.

13. <u>SAMURAI:</u> Expert swordsmen who train to master their fear. The "KATANA" sword brings out the potential.

14. <u>NINJA:</u> Fighting enemies in darkness, they pursue their mission without fear of death. They can throw weapons like sharp stars.

When the "Flame of Creation" finished up giving Igworm all the information about the Warrior Job List, Igworm started to stare at the "Flame of Creation" and then after said out of curiosity, "How do you know so much about this WARRIOR JOB LIST? Is their ANOTHER soul in you besides the ones in the past like King Scarecrow and Queen Sandra"? The "Flame of Creation" paused for a while and later said to Igworm, "Such powerful questions Igworm, very powerful questions indeed. But like I said before, time will tell AFTER everything is finished up HERE, you won't be disappointed".

Igworm just stared at what the "Flame of Creation" just said to him. Soon after Igworm said with a glare, "Tell me, how do I decide which half to pick? Will you help me"? "No, I am not allow to help you, only YOU can decide half of the Warrior Jobs, sorry", said the "Flame of Creation".

CHAPTER 20

KING GOBBY AND KING VICTOR– HOW LONG FOR BATTLE?

It had to be about five hours more when King Gobby and King Victor returned to the Kingdom of Hydra with the breaking news, very bad news and it happen on the burial day of King Scarecrow.

"We will rest for the rest of the day everyone. Thank-you for all your help and we will continue tomorrow. Myself, King Gobby, the village leader, the tribal leader and the head of the Mermen are very grateful, THANK-YOU ALL", said King Victor. After saying that, everyone clapped and went home to rest. The creatures, the Mermen and the Gob-wings remained in the village part of the Kingdom (because their homes is far away, too long of a distance).

"So, my friend Gobby, how long for battle? Any rough guesses"? said King Victor. King Gobby looked up at King Victor, very tired and very sad at the same time, "I think it will take Iggy and Wormy to reach the Kingdom of Hydra in about four days tops. The "Flame of Creation", I think, is much stronger then the last one". "FOUR DAYS? But it takes time to make an army, look at King Scarecrow and his minions of Grave Diggers in the past, so that I have read", said King Victor. King Gobby took a deep breathe and said, "Like I said Victor, the "Flame of Creation" is much stronger then the last one. I could be wrong but I think someone or SOMETHING else is at play here instead of Iggy and Wormy". "WHO"? said King Victor. "I will tell you tomorrow and it is just an educational guess but right now we need rest", said King Gobby. "Of course", said King Victor, patting King Gobby on the shoulder.

CHAPTER 21

IGWORM-WARRIOR JOBS CHOSEN

"So many to chose from and so little time as well", said Igworm. "You are right", said the "Flame of Creation". "Have you made your decision, Igworm? Because like you said so-little time", added the "Flame of Creation". "Don't rush me. HA, HA, HA," laughed Igworm.

Igworm walked a bit in the cave for a while, then turned around to look at the waterfall and then back at the "Flame of Creation". "I have made my decision", said Igworm. " Finally, which seven of the fourteen have you chosen for your new species, Igworm", said the "Flame of Creation". Igworm said, "I have chosen

Chemist, Knight, Archer, White Mage, Black Mage, Samurai and Summoner". "I think they are very good choices you have made Igworm", said the " Flame of Creation".

"THANK-YOU VERY MUCH", shouted Igworm, very excited about the whole manner. "There is one more thing I forgot to mention to you, Igworm" said the "Flame of Creation". "And what is that"? said Igworm, still excited. "In order for you to acquire these seven Warrior Jobs, you have to destroy the "Flame of Creation". The reason is because the Warrior Jobs have power and so does the sword, you can't have TWO, only ONE, which will it be then- the Warrior Jobs OR the "Flame of Creation'? But remember, either way, your new species can use the weapons by the Warrior Jobs you have chosen. What is your decision, Igworm"? Igworm grinned and said, "WARRIOR JOBS"! "So be it then", said the "Flame of Creation".

CHAPTER 22

KING GOBBY AND KING VICTOR– POSSIBLE THIRD SOUL

By early the next morning, after everyone had their breakfast, King Gobby said to King Victor, the village leader, the tribal leader and the head of the Mermen, "I have something to tell all of you, so please, hurry up and meet me in the throne room, please". Everyone looked at each other, confused and puzzled.

As everyone gather in the throne room, King Gobby stood up and said, "Before I went to sleep last night, I said to Victor here that there might be a possibility that someone else is at play here, maybe a third soul and that soul could be my brother Hope", "WHAT", said King Victor, "I thought that it was his idea to create the "Flame of Creation", along with the other creatures powers in the afterlife to bring peace and balance". "It is only a guess Victor and I could be wrong but when I think about it even more, when King Scarecrow drove the "Flame of Creation" into Hope, at that moment, MAYBE some of Hope's soul went into the sword AFTER Hope disappeared and screamed at the same time," said King Gobby.

Everyone nodded their heads up and down. "But I really believe Hope is not the enemy, just a theory. I believe that the power of the "Flame of Creation" went to Iggy's and Wormy's heads. If it is true what I am saying about a third soul into the "Flame of Creation", I really believe Hope will help us and not against us, a trick up his sleeve if you want to call it", said King Gobby. "I "HOPE" you are right, Gobby", said King Victor, as the village leader, the tribal leader and the head of the Mermen nodded their heads, in complete silence the whole time, not saying a word.

CHAPTER 23

IGWORM-R.I.P. "FLAME OF CREATION"

The "Flame of Creation" glowing even more brighter then ever, Igworm pick up the sword at hand and said, "How do I destroy you"? The "Flame of Creation", glowing even MORE purple then ever said, "To destroy the "Flame of Creation", you have to say the Lord's Prayer". "And what is this prayer"? said Igworm. "I will tell you the Lord's Prayer like I did about the Warrior Jobs List. After I finished telling you the prayer, say it back to the "Flame of Creation" and the sword can rest in peace, OK"? The "Flame of Creation" shot out a beam of purple light and went right into Igworm's head. A few minutes later, the "Flame of Creation" stopped the beam. Then Igworm repeated the Lord's Prayer back at the "Flame of Creation". With that, the sword turn grey, white as a ghost, then turn to ash and vanish into thin air.

Igworm bow down his head, out of respect, then said, "Rest in peace, "Flame of Creation", you have been very useful and very helpful, I will not let you down OR myself down for that matter".

Igworm then walked out of the entrance of the waterfall and said, "I have to get to the gates of the Kingdom of Hydra but how? I know, I will track the scent of that creature Gobby and Victor hitched a ride on, it will take me right to them, along with my new species, my new ARMY, HA, HA, HA".

CHAPTER 24

KING GOBBY AND KING VICTOR- FOUR DAYS LEFT FOR WAR PART 1

About two hours later..... "Only four days left to war", said King Victor, as he was beginning to worry about the whole situation. King Gobby heard what King Victor said, walked over to him and said, "You are right, only four days left for war and the last one too". King Victor looked back at King Gobby and said, "You sound pretty sure of yourself about being the "last one", my friend". "There is so much the "Flame of Creation" can take and I think this is the last one, I can only pray so", said King Gobby.

King Victor looked out at one of the throne room windows and saw everyone working getting ready for battle-for war. After King Victor turned around to look at King Gobby, then said to him after, "You said something about a third soul, YES"? "I DID say that but I could be wrong",said King Gobby. "And Iggy and Wormy also said that THEY can bring back King Scarecrow back to life, saying that WE can pick whoever we want when the time is right"? "That's what they both said to us but I find it hard to believe but...", King Gobby stopped with a paused. "But what"? said King Victor. King Gobby continued, "The "Flame of Creation" WAS created in the afterlife by the creatures power, along with my brothers power Hope, and King Scarecrow is half creature, you see. So maybe Iggy and Wormy are telling the truth about King Scarecrow coming back to life, back from the dead. There are rules with the "Flame of Creation" and ONLY Iggy and Wormy knows them but that knowledge is too great. Maybe that is WHY both Iggy and Wormy are like they are, confused......maybe poisoned, you know".

King Victor said after, "Maybe you are right, my friend. But I hope King Scarecrow comes back to life to aid us all, that would be a huge benefit. If someone knows the "Flame of Creation", it is King Scarecrow". "You couldn't put it better then myself. Now, lets go outside and give everyone a helping hand", said King Gobby. "That's a good idea", said King Victor.

CHAPTER 25

IGWORM-FOUR DAYS LEFT TO WAR PART 2

"The scent of that creature Gobby and Victor hitched a ride on is getting stronger. It could be the same one OR there could be others around, only time will tell, HA, HA, HA", laughed Igworm.

Igworm must have walked about three hours after leaving the entrance of the waterfall. Igworm said to himself, "The "Flame of Creation" is now resting at the waterfall. How about I call that waterfall, "Flame of Creation Falls", I think it has a good sharp-edge on it, ha, ha". Soon after Igworm heard a noise up ahead and he was right, there was a Gob-wing close by. It looks like the Gob-wing is collecting some wood to return to the Kingdom of Hydra. Just as the Gob-wing was about to leave, Igworm jumped on him, wrapped his arm around the Gob-wings neck and crack it. "You weren't so tough after all, HA, HA, HA", laughed Igworm, looking down on the corpse of the Gob-wing.

Igworm just stared at the Gob-wing and later said, "Your wings look very interesting. Along with your peck and talons".

Igworm soon rip the Gob-wing's wings off the body and got some vines nearby. Tied them on his back . The same thing for the peck and talons, Igworm tied both of these around his neck. "I think my new look will impress Gobby and Victor, HA, HA, HA", laughed Igworm, as he continued walking, leaving the dead corpse of the Gob-wing behind.

CHAPTER 26

KING GOBBY AND KING VICTOR- THREE DAYS TO WAR PART 3

It was around ten in the morning and the tribal leader came running in the throne room and said to both King Gobby and King Victor, "I ask one of the Gob-wings to go and collect some wood to make some bows-n-arrows and NEVER return and that was yesterday, around noon", said the tribal leader. King Gobby and King Victor looked at each other then back at the tribal leader, "Nine chances out of ten, that Gob-wing is dead", said King Victor. "WHAT!", said the tribal leader. King Gobby put his hand on the tribal leader's shoulder and said to him, "Victor is probably right. Maybe Iggy and Wormy killed that Gob-wing. Maybe when the Gob-wing had its back turned, Iggy and Wormy jumped him and killed him". "That coward", said the tribal leader, very angry for the moment.

The village leader overheard the conversation and later said, "How about we sent a flock of Gob-wings after Iggy and Wormy"?. "Good idea", said the head of the Mermen, coming in from behind the village leader. "That would not do any help. We have to focus on their NEW minions and I hope it is not the Grave Diggers", said King Victor, raising his eyebrows at King Gobby. King Gobby smiled and later said, "Victor is right, we will continue to get ready for war and it is only a few more days anyway. Besides, we need EVERYONE here. We need everyone to concentrate on the task ahead".

After that said everyone got something to eat, went back to work, to protect for what they all have fought for five-hundred years ago against King Scarecrow and his Grave Diggers.

CHAPTER 27

IGWORM-THREE DAYS LEFT TO WAR PART 4

It was around noon, Igworm, who is very tired of walking the distance, said to himself, "It was yesterday that I killed that creature. I should have taking some of the creatures meat to eat along the way but I guess it is meant to be, it wouldn't have taste good. But I guess fear is rising at the Kingdom of Hydra, when they notice that there precious creature didn't return home to them with their lovely wood, HA, HA, HA," laughed Igworm.

Still following the scent of the Gob-wing, Igworm heard someone up ahead. Igworm poked out his head out of the bushes and saw a different creature, not a Gob-wing. It looked like a child-creature playing by herself. How Igworm know it was a girl is because the way she was dressed up. She was playing with her dolls like a tea-party or something.

Igworm got out of the bushes, walked over to her and said, "Which way to the Kingdom of Hydra, GIRL"? The little girl-creature stopped playing with her dolls, looked up at Igworm, not afraid and then said to him, "It is about three days walk, that way sir". "You are not afraid of me, WHY"? said Igworm. "Why should I be. You haven't wrong me or anyone else for that matter", said the little girl-creature. "Not yet, HA, HA, HA", laughed Igworm, as he continued to walk away form the little girl-creature. Igworm turned around to look at the little girl-creature, while walking and all she did is continue again to play with her dolls.

CHAPTER 28

KING GOBBY AND KING VICTOR–
TWO DAYS LEFT TO WAR
PART 5

"I think everyone was on edge yesterday, Gobby", said King Victor. "I know", said King Gobby. "Ever since everyone found out about that Gob-wing didn't return with the wood, everyone started to lose a bit of confidence, in a way and I can't blame them, not one little bit. Gob-wings are big creatures, pretty hard to take down if you ask me, Gobby", said King Victor, getting mad. "You know what I call this Victor"? said King Gobby, "What"?

said King Victor. "Motivated, adding wood to the fire, if you mess with a bull you will get the horn, right"? said King Gobby.

King Victor said, "Your right". "I know I am right. Our job is to "MOTIVATE" our people. Iggy and Wormy made their first mistake for killing that Gob-wing, think about it, they are getting sloppy, right at the starting line, BEFORE the battle",said King Gobby.

King Victor grinned at King Gobby and said, "Before everyone starts to work, WE, US, TOGETHER, will tell everyone this. I don't want the creatures, the people, the Mermen and the Gob-wings fallen member lose spirit. It is nine in the morning and we all have a busy day ahead of us all, my friend". Gobby smiled and said, "I see Josiah in you Victor, he was and still IS a wonderful man. I know you won't let him down including myself ".

Both King Gobby and King Victor put one arm on each others shoulders, grinned and walked out of the throne room together.

CHAPTER 29

IGWORM-TWO DAYS LEFT TO WAR PART 6

Morning came again for Igworm, very tired and very angry about walking the distance each day. By noon, to started to rain. Igworm started to think about this little girl-creature and said to himself, "She wasn't afraid of me but the strangest part of all, WHY, why was she playing with her dolls, in the middle of nowhere, into the wild, by HERSELF? Something is definitely not right about that".

It was raining hard, very hard in the afternoon. Igworm stood under a tall tree, waiting for the rain to stop coming down hard or slack-off a bit so Igworm can continue his way towards the Kingdom of Hydra.

After a while the rain stopped completely. "It is about time", said Igworm, very angry for the moment. Soon after Igworm heard a noise behind him. It was that little girl-creature. "Hello sir, we meet again", she said. "What do you want? Why are you following me? Who are you"? shouted Igworm. "Don't get angry sir, I just wanted to give you one of my dolls, for company. The road is long sir and maybe this doll will boost your spirits up, that's all", said the little girl-creature.

"I don't need a stupid doll for company, GO AWAY", shouted Igworm. And with that, the little girl-creature disappeared right in front of Igworm's eyes, leaving one the doll behind. Igworm just stared down at the doll, pick it up and said to himself, "Thank-you "Flame of Creation", I guess I will keep this doll after all then".

CHAPTER 30

KING GOBBY AND KING VICTOR-
ONE DAY LEFT TO WAR
PART 7

It was around eight in the morning, King Victor was pacing back and forth in the throne room, saying to himself, "Tomorrow is war, I can't believe it". "You better believe it", said King Gobby. King Victor turned around quickly to look at King Gobby.

"Cup of tea'? said King Victor. "Yes please", said King Gobby. "I have a question for you Gobby"? said King Victor. King Gobby took a mouthful of tea and answered, "And what is that, my friend"? King Victor pick up his cup of tea, took a sip and said, "Iggy and Wormy mentioned in the past that they can fuse together with the power of the "Flame of Creation". We can bring someone back to life, like King Scarecrow. I wonder if it is possible to do that".

King Gobby leaned back in his chair and said, "Like I said in the past Victor, anything is possible with the "Flame of Creation", ANYTHING". "I was also thinking about that Gob-wing. What IF Iggy and Wormy fuse together and killed that Gob-wing. Do you remember what Iggy and Wormy said that if they fuse together they would call themselves "Igworm", do you remember Gobby"? said King Victor. "Yes, I remember", said King Gobby. "But you have a really good point about the fusing part but I don't know how WE can bring back King Scarecrow from the dead",added King Gobby. "Victor said shortly, "Lets just finish our tea and make the finishing touches on today's work. By tomorrow, MAYBE, we can bring King Scarecrow back to aid us in battle, if anyway possible like a miracle". "True", said King Gobby, as both of them finished up their cups of tea and walked out the throne room.

CHAPTER 31

IGWORM-ONE DAY LEFT TO WAR PART 8

When the little girl-creature disappeared yesterday up until now, Igworm was just thinking about that moment. As for the doll the little girl-creature left behind, Igworm just stared at it while walking, getting even closer at the gates of the Kingdom of Hydra.

It had to be around twenty-four hours since the little girl-creature disappeared into thin air. Just of a sudden, something appeared in front of the doll. Igworm stopped walking, came to an halt. It was a piece of paper. Igworm read it and it said, "This doll looks exactly like one of King Scarecrow's Grave Diggers. They are the very half-human and half-creatures that fought five-hundred years ago and now they are extinct. But remember, even though they fought bravery. The reason why I am telling you and gave you this doll is because even enemies can show respect at the end of the day, just remember that. I wish you the best of luck in battle and hope for the best at the end of the day"-"Flame of Creation". P.S.-"Thank-you for naming that waterfall after me, I am grateful for that".

"Knew it", said Igworm. "This doll IS from the "Flame of Creation" and by the sound of things, it looks like the "Flame of Creation"what's me to win this war. Well, at least I have someone or should I say SOMETHING on my side. Just one more day and it will be CRUNCH TIME for Gobby and Victor, just like the creature I am wearing on my back and around my neck, HA, HA, HA", laughed Igworm.

CHAPTER 32

KING GOBBY AND KING VICTOR– MYSTERIOUS LIGHT

As everyone was getting ready for battle, King Victor said to King Gobby, "Gobby, when do you think Iggy and Wormy will be here"? "An educational guess, in about five to seven hours but I see no army of such", said King Gobby, very confused at this point. "That is why I ask you because like you said Gobby, NOBODY sees an army in the distance", said King Victor, even more confused then King Gobby.

King Victor ask everyone to meet at the center of the town square. Everyone did what King Victor ask them to do. When King Victor got to the center of the towns square, along with King Gobby, the village leader, the tribal leader and the head of the Mermen, King Victor stood on a platform and said to everyone, "EVERYONE, people, creatures, Mermen and Gob-wings, your efforts will be remembered for all time, your efforts for working well with each other is a sight that we will win this war and win the freedom that we all fought so hard for in the past, five-hundred years ago. Now lets show this enemy what we are made of, ready your positions and finally, don't fail yourselves, THANK-YOU".

With that everyone cheered. "You couldn't have put it better then myself", said King Gobby. Soon after there was a bright light shining inside and outside the castle. Everyone stopped cheering and stared at the mysterious light.

A SURPRISED GUEST BACK FROM THE GRAVE

King Victor said to everyone, "You all wait here. Only myself, King Gobby, the village leader, the tribal leader and the head of the Mermen will go to the castle with me. I want some soldiers at the castle as well". With that, King Gobby, King Victor and the rest of them rush to the castle to investigate the mysterious, bright light.

When they all enter the castle, the mysterious bright light vanished, out of sight. "I wonder what that light was"? said the village leader. "Maybe it is a sign of victory, from a higher place", added the tribal leader. "I think it is a sign from the "Flame of Creation", telling all of us we are already victorious", added the head of the Mermen.

"You are ALL wrong but good answers, I must say", said a strange voice. "Who are you"? said King Victor. "Now, now, now, King Victor. Is that how you answer a old friend like that'? said the strange voice again. "We would not know because we can only hear you, not see you", said King Gobby.

Hiding behind King Victor's throne chair, the mysterious person or WHATEVER, got up, and walked in front of them. King Gobby, King Victor, the village leader, the tribal leader, the head of the Mermen and the soldiers, all of them in total, complete shock of WHO stood in front of them. His body looked very skinny, very tall, his arms looked deformed, his face very scary looking, his hair looked like hay, wearing long, brown, leather boots, and a salt-n-pepper hat on his head.

<u>KING SCARECROW IS BACK!</u>

<u>TO BE CONCLUDED!</u>

IGGY AND WORMY– PART 2

INTRO

In this third and final part of this series, it left off where King Scarecrow is back from the dead and faces King Gobby, King Victor and the rest of them in the throne room in the Kingdom of Hydra.

How did King Scarecrow come back to life? King Gobby and King Victor didn't do ANYTHING to bring back King Scarecrow. And what does King Scarecrow have to say? Is it good? OR is it bad news? Only time will tell.

CHAPTER 34

THE RETURN OF KING SCARECROW

 King Gobby, King Victor, the village leader, the tribal leader, the head of the Mermen and the soldiers just stood there, in complete silence and total shock all at once to see right in front of them, the very man they have buried about five days ago.

"So, did you all miss me?", said King Scarecrow, with a small grin on his face. "It was only about five days ago but it seem to me it was about five YEARS but, "YES", WE did miss you", said King Gobby. "Likewise", said King Victor, as everyone else present in the throne room nodded their heads up and down.

"So how did you come back from the dead, King Scarecrow?", said the village leader. "Both Gobby and Victor did", said King Scarecrow. "How"? said the tribal leader.

King Scarecrow walked closer towards them all and said, "Gobby's and Victor's hearts were set on me of whoever they want back here in this time, to help you fight this war against Igworm". "Igworm"?, said the head of the Merman. "That is right, my friend. Iggy and Wormy fused themselves together and gave them a NEW name, Igworm".

And again complete silence. "How did you know about Iggy and Wormy fusing together?", said King Victor. "I am part of the "Flame of Creation", remember. My soul is part of that sword, along with Queen Sandra and Hope" said King Scarecrow. "Makes sense", said King Gabby.

Soon after, everyone went over and hugged King Scarecrow and welcomed him back. "I have so much to tell you so you all better sit down and listen to what I have to say. King Victor, if you don't mind telling your guard soldiers here to tell everyone that I am back, maybe to ease a bit of tension, after all, war is only a few hours away", said King Scarecrow. "Good idea", said King Victor. King Victor commanded the guard soldiers to tell everyone the good news about King Scarecrow returning from the grave and helping everyone fight this war against Igworm and his minions of Iggy's and Wormy's. "So much to tell, so little time", said King Scarecrow, showing worry on his face. Everyone else started to look worry as well. King Gobby went over to King Scarecrow, patted him on the shoulder and said to him, out of concern and a smile to go with it, "We are all here with you till the end. You help us and we will help you, Ok?" "Thank-you", said King Scarecrow, "You are a TRUE friend, indeed".

CHAPTER 35

SIX HOURS LEFT TO WAR–
THIRD SOUL REVEALED

"OK", said King Scarecrow, "I will begin with the sword, the "Flame of Creation". The "Flame of Creation" was guiding Igworm right from the beginning up until now". King Scarecrow took a deep breathe and continued. "Like I said before my soul is part of the "Flame of Creation" just like Queen Sandra and Hope. In order to complete the task ahead and destroy the "Flame of Creation" forever, myself, Queen Sandra and Hope must see this through". "Why destroy it, I mean the "Flame of Creation", WHY?", said King Victor. "Because, my friend, there is only so much the sword can take", said King Scarecrow. "Exactly what said in the past", said King Gobby. "As I was saying, all three of us has to take part of this task. Even though if we didn't like it OR didn't want to do it, it must be done-in order to free the three of us from the "Flame of Creation" and get peace again that we all rightfully deserve. The voice guiding Igworm and helping him is Hope. He didn't want to do it BUT Hope had no choice, the "Flame of Creation" told him to do it in order to be free from this madness and war. So Hope agree to it. Hope is only asking you all to understand his position he is in, that is all-sorry", said King Scarecrow. "Like I said in the past, there was a possibility my brother is in this mess but myself and everyone here understands-he is forgiven-AGAIN", said King Gobby, smiling.

CHAPTER 36

FIVE AND A HALF HOURS LEFT TO WAR— NEW BODY

King Scarecrow continued with his story among the others. "At the waterfall, the very place I have killed the fake Scarecrow AND myself transformed into Scarecrow, Iggy and Wormy were deciding if they both find a way to make peace with us all-creatures, Merman and human-beings alike. But the power went to their heads so they both killed each other with their own hands by slicing each others throats. Soon after that, they both fell down on the ground and bled to death". "Soon after both souls of Iggy and Wormy left their bodies. The bodies lying on the ground disappeared into thin air. As for the souls that left the bodies, covered in blood, both souls went into each other to form a NEW soul and a NEW body. The new body look like Wormy but the skin color look like Iggy, more blue then any other color on him. He named himself Igworm because Iggy is short for "IG" and Wormy is short for "WORM", put them both together and you get "IGWORM".

"Igworm has the same facial features as Iggy and Wormy but a lot taller and stronger as well", said King Scarecrow, taking a breather.

King Gobby, King Victor, and everyone else just stared at King Scarecrow and later back at each other wandering what King Scarecrow is going to say next.

CHAPTER 37

FIVE HOURS LEFT TO WAR-NEW WEAPONS

"Next I will tell you about Igworms new weapons, for the moment", continued King Scarecrow. "After Igworm got his new body, a brand-new "Flame of Creation" appeared right in front of Igworm. The "Flame of Creation" was a bright-purple color looking sword, it was a beautiful sword if you ask me".

"What do you mean Scarecrow that it "WAS" a beautiful sword?", said King Gobby. "I will tell you that part later, OK?", said King Scarecrow, with a sad look on his face. Everyone, at that moment, looked at each other-puzzled.

"The "Flame of Creation" said to Igworm that there are benefits with the sword like making weapons, making soldiers and also different classes to chose but I will get to that later on as well".

King Scarecrow looked over at King Gobby and asked him, "Do you know what time it is, Gobby?". "It is about two o'clock in the afternoon, why do you ask?", said King Gobby, very curious for the moment. "I only have a few more hours left and later I have to leave you all- FOREVER", said King Scarecrow.

Everyone looked at each other. Later King Victor said, "Where do you have to go, Scarecrow?" King Scarecrow answered back to King Victor, smiling, "I will tell you in a few hours, my friend".

CHAPTER 38

FOUR AND A HALF HOURS LEFT TO WAR- NEW MINIONS

"Now I will tell you all about Igworm's new minions, his new species or should I say his new army", said King Scarecrow, as he sat back in his chair and both of his hands on the back of his head. "Igworm's new breed look exactly like Iggy and Wormy. Two hundred and fifty thousand Iggy's and the same amount for the Wormy's, two hundred and fifty thousand. A grand total of five hundred thousand minions at the doorstep, at the gates of the Kingdom of Hydra". "Igworms's army is outside right now as I am telling you all this. They are ALL underground. When Igworm arrives here at the gates, they will ALL come up and be ready for battle. Heavily armed-helmets, thick armor and strong shields to go with it as well", said King Scarecrow, shaking head left and right.

"I knew it",said the head of the Mermen, "I said that our enemy is waiting for us just outside the gates. I said that they are already there waiting". "Yes, you did say that head Mermen", said King Gobby. Everyone else nodded their heads up and down, agreeing what the head of the Mermen just said.

"Is there anything else you have to tell us, Scarecrow?", said King Gobby raising his eyebrows. King Scarecrow looked over at King Gobby, smiling, "OH YES". " Is there any good news at all, King Scarecrow?", said King Victor. "Some", said King Scarecrow, "But that part is for the very last, trust me, you all won't be disappointed", smiled King Scarecrow.

CHAPTER 39

FOUR HOURS LEFT TO WAR- WEAPON MAKING

"Now I am going to tell you about the weapons Hope made for Igworm. And again Hope didn't want to do it, the "Flame of Creation" told Hope to do it. Again there are rules when you are part of the "Flame of Creation" and if you don't obey those rules, there will be a penalty, I hope you all understand, my friends", said King Scarecrow. "We all understand Scarecrow. Hope is doing his part, just like you", said King Victor. "Thank-you", said King Scarecrow. "The weapons Hope made for Igworm are swords, helmets, shields, maces, spears, potions, staffs, tridents, bows-n-arrows, knives, strong armor, sharp-stars, magic and the most strongest weapon of all- the "Katana" sword", said King Scarecrow. "How can they ALL use these weapons, I mean, to perfect their abilities and skills in a short amount of time?", said King Victor.

King Scarecrow grinned at King Victor, "With the power of the "Flame of Creation", ANYTHING is possible", said King Scarecrow. Everyone nodded their heads up and down, agreeing with what King Scarecrow have just said to them all.

"Only three and a half hours left for me to concluded everything with you all. I hope my information is being very helpful to you, said King Scarecrow, smiling. "It is indeed", said King Gobby, smiling back at King Scarecrow, giving him a wink in the process.

CHAPTER 40

THREE AND A HALF HOURS LEFT TO WAR- "WARRIOR JOB LIST"

"This next part I am about to tell you all will raise a lot of concerns, make you raise your eyebrows and make you open your eyes wide OPEN", said King Scarecrow, with a serious look on his face. "This is called the "Warrior Job List". It is a list of different warrior classes throughout time and space, where the "Flame of Creation"got this information, I truly do not know. Anyway, back to the subject at hand on the "Warrior Job List", there is fourteen classes altogether and Igworm can pick seven out of the fourteen of them. The names of the fourteen classes are:1-Knight, 2-Archer, 3-Squire, 4-Chemist, 5-Monk, 6-White Mage, 7-Black Mage, 8-Time Mage, 9-Summoner, 10-Thief, 11-Geomancer, 12-Lancer, 13-Ninja, 14-Samurai. That's all of them", said King Scarecrow.

And again everyone in complete silence and complete shock at the same time. "We are in serious trouble", said the village leader. "I agree with you, one-hundred percent", said the tribal leader. "But we have combat and tactical experience, this breed of minions have NONE",replied the head of the Mermen.

King Gobby and King Victor looked at each other and after back at King Scarecrow. King Gobby stood up and said to King Scarecrow, "Would you like a cup of tea, Scarecrow?". "Yes please", said King Scarecrow. King Gobby handed over a cup of tea to King Scarecrow, as well with the others. "Continued, please", said King Gobby. King Scarecrow answered back, "Thank-you".

CHAPTER 41

THREE HOURS LEFT TO WAR-
WARRIOR JOBS CHOSEN

King Scarecrow pick up his cup of tea, took a mouthful to clear his throat and continued his information about Igworm and the "Flame of Creation" with King Gobby, King Victor, the village leader, the tribal leader and the head of the Mermen.

"The Warrior Jobs Igworm has chosen are: 1-Chemist-they are experts with potions, 2-Knights, 3-Archers, 4-White Mage-they can heal and protect everybody's surroundings, 5-Black Mage-they can use a variety of different element magic, 6-Samurai-they can use the most powerful weapon at hand-the "Katana", and finally 7-Summoner-they can summon ONE beast from the other side only once and it is a one-shot-deal as well. It can be any element-Thunder, Fire, Water, Ice OR Earth. Which one will they pick, I have NO idea until the time comes", said King Scarecrow.

King Victor stood up, walked towards one of the windows in the throne room and looked out. King Victor saw everyone outside, in a way, celebrating because of the news that King Scarecrow came back from the dead. King Victor later walked back to join the rest, sat down and said, "So, is there any good news for us human-beings, creatures and Mermen?".

King Scarecrow took another mouthful of tea and said, "Yes, but before I get to that part, I will tell all the saddest part of my story with you all". Everyone looked at King Scarecrow like he had ten heads or something.

CHAPTER 42

TWO AND A HALF HOURS LEFT TO WAR– R.I.P. "FLAME OF CREATION"

"This next part I am about to tell all of you is about the "Flame of Creation". Igworm was given a choice which is use the use the power of the "Flame of Creation" OR keep the Warrior Jobs he has chosen for his new breed of species. Igworm was also told by Hope that whichever one he has chosen, his minions can use the weapons he has chosen from the "Warrior Job List". Now that does not necessary mean Igworms army would be masters or experts with these weapons in hand but they can USE them, that is all. So Igworm has chosen the Warrior Jobs he has picked for his army", said King Scarecrow.

King Scarecrow took a short paused and said, "The "Flame of Creation" OR Hope said to Igworm if you want the Warrior Jobs, you have to destroy the "Flame of Creation" and by doing that Igworm has to say the Lord's Prayer to the sword. So Hope put the Lord's Prayer inside Igworms head and ask him to repeat it back at the sword, word-for-word. And so Igworm did what he was told and a few minutes later, the "Flame of Creation" turned white as a ghost and a gray-like color. Soon it turn into ash and vanished into thin air. Now there is NO MORE "Flame of Creation" gentlemen and that concludes my story up until NOW. I hope my information was useful to you all", said King Scarecrow.

"Like I said to you Victor, this is going to be the LAST war-FOREVER, didn't I say that to you?", said King Gobby. "Yes, you did and I am sorry for doubting you, forgive me", said King Victor, with a bow. "No hard feelings", said King Gobby, as he bow back at King Victor, smiling.

CHAPTER 43

TWO HOURS LEFT TO WAR-GOOD NEWS

"NOW", said King Scarecrow, very excited for the moment, while everyone just stared at King Scarecrow, puzzled with war drawing very near. "I have good news for you all and it is the part Queen Sandra played in. Hope's part is to help Igworm, my part is to tell everyone of you what went down at the waterfall, at the farm plains of Eternal. Finally Queen Sandra's part, which is what she gave Igworm and that my friends is a doll".

"A doll?", said King Victor, puzzled and confused, along with everyone else. "That's right", said King Scarecrow. "On the way to the

Kingdom of Hydra, Igworm met a little girl-creature. In disguise it was Queen Sandra and she gave Igworm a doll. This doll is no ordinary doll-it is a special doll, it looks like a Grave Digger. It is myself, Hope's and Queen Sandra's symbol of freedom and peace".

King Scarecrow stood up and said out of concern, "How many soldiers do you ALL have altogether?". "About half of what Igworm has", said King Victor. "Myself and Victor tried to foul Igworm, who was Iggy and Wormy back then, that we had the same amount of soldiers but that plan back-fired on us as you can see", said King Gobby, red in the face (embarrass for the moment).

"No worries because Queen Sandra can even up the odds for all of you. All Igworm has to do is drop the doll on the ground at the city gates and up will come out of the very earth is two hundred and fifty thousand Grave Diggers to fight by your side".

"WHAT!", said King Gobby. "That is right. It is Queen Sandra's gift for all of you, they will not disappointed you all in battle, my friends",smiled King Scarecrow, as he went over to each one and patted them on the shoulder.

CHAPTER 44

ONE AND A HALF HOUR LEFT TO WAR— KING SCARECROW TAKES HIS LEAVE

"Here comes the sad part", said King Scarecrow, smiling at everyone. "And what is that, Scarecrow?", said King Gobby. King Scarecrow walked over toward King Gobby, still smiling and said to him, "I have to return to the afterlife, my friend. I was sent here by the "Flame of Creation" to complete the task which is what I have done, along with Hope and Queen Sandra. WE completed the task and NOW all three of us are free from the bonds by the power of the "Flame of Creation". Finally all three of us can rest in peace and harmony and not be attached to the madness of that sword".

"You are right about one thing, King Gobby", said King Scarecrow. "And what is that?", said King Gobby, tears rolling down his face. "You said I would be grateful for the form King Josiah gave me, by looking like a "scarecrow" and you are right. I am greatly blessed and I thank-you for that, King Gobby. After all it was your powers that gave me the form", said King Scarecrow. Still smiling, as he walked over to each one of them, gave them all a hug and kissed them on the head.

"Good-bye my dear friends. Tell everyone outside I love them all and wish them the very best of luck in battle from myself, Hope and Queen Sandra. I will see you all on the other side down the road, take care", said King Scarecrow. With that, King Scarecrow glowed a bright light blue and disappeared right in front of everyone.

King Gobby, King Victor, the village leader, the tribal leader and the head of the Mermen bow their heads down, in respect to King Scarecrow, former King of the Mermen, in complete silence.

CHAPTER 45

ONE HOUR LEFT TO WAR– GETTING READY FOR BATTLE

"We all have one hour left for battle and Igworm will be here soon so we better get ready, shall we?", said King Gobby, wiping the tears off his face.

"I will tell everyone what went down here", said King Victor. "Good idea", said the village leader. "I will get everyone ready themselves up for battle", said the tribal leader. "I will get everyone to ready themselves into their positions", said the head of the Mermen.

"We all have a task to do, just like King Scarecrow, Queen Sandra and Hope did. Lets not fail them, they did their part, NOW, lets do our part", said King Gobby, as everyone in the throne room cheered and clamp.

King Victor and the village leader went to the towns square first with some guard soldiers and told everyone brief of what happen inside the castle at the throne room. While the tribal leader and the head of the Mermen got every strong lad and soldier to ready their positions. King Gobby, on the other hand, was outside by the gates, just staring straight ahead at the flat open plains.

After a while, King Gobby said to himself, "My time is very near, my friend Scarecrow. I will see you soon and be with the other creatures in the afterlife too. But there as to be a weakness to Igworm and his minions but WHAT? I will figure it out, I will not disappoint and let you down King Scarecrow".

CHAPTER 46

IGWORM DRAWS NEAR

Later on for a while, King Gobby saw someone or SOMETHING, very tall and huge walking towards the gates of the Kingdom of Hydra. "So that must be Igworm", said King Gobby, talking to himself again.

King Gobby went back inside the castle gates and shouted out loud, "READY YOUR POSITIONS, IGWORM WILL BE HERE SOON. HE IS ONLY A DISTANCE AWAY".

With that said, everyone rush towards outside the city gates, ready all archers, soldiers,

Mermen, creatures and YES, even the Gob-wings were ready as well.

It took no-time for everyone to get ready. Everyone saw Igworm getting even closer, the closer Igworm came towards them, the taller and larger he seem to them. Everyone also notice that Igworm has wings on his back, they are wings from a Gob-wing. "That must be the Gob-wing I sent to get us some wood so we can make bows-n-arrows", said the tribal leader, angry for the moment. King Gobby, King Victor, the village leader and the head of the Mermen nodded their heads up and down, agreeing of what the tribal leader just said.

Igworm took a few more steps and stopped. Igworm was about a hundred feet away from everyone, smiling at them all, a very cruel smile indeed. "Do you all like my new look. I think it SUITS me, don't you think?", said Igworm, laughing. "YOU COWARD", shouted the tribal leader. 'We shall see about that", said Igworm, looking very serious for the moment.

CHAPTER 47

IGWORMS NEW BREED OF MINIONS

"HA, HA, HA, is this it? Kingdom of Hydra's powerhouse? I have half a million minions and YOU have about half of the number of mine. Well, well, well, I am insulted. I call forth all of you- IGGY'S and WORMY'S-to fight on my side and claim this country for ourselves, HA, HA, HA", laughed Igworm. A few minutes later, up came from the ground-half Iggy's and half Wormy's-heavily armed and armored. They all look like the Warrior Jobs Igworm has chosen-Knights, Archers, Chemists, White Mages, Black Mages,

Samurai's and Summoners-ALL OF THEM-ready to spill blood for Igworm.

King Gobby, King Victor and rest of them could not believe their eyes of what happen a few minutes ago. King Victor walked a bit closer to Igworm and said, "Myself and the rest of us are not afraid you Igworm and I tell you ALL now if you don't surrender right NOW, WE won't show any mercy-NONE-what-so-ever. Do I make myself CRYSTAL CLEAR".

Igworm answered back, "I was hoping you would say that, old buddy, HA, HA, HA. Plus I love a good challenge, along with my new breed of killing machines right here, don't you agree?". "Like I said back in the waterfall area, we will hit you hard and make you run, like mice and I guess I can add in jackrabbits too, OLD BUDDY", said King Victor. Igworm took a few steps ahead and said, "I would love to see that happen", glared Igworm.

CHAPTER 48

GRAVE DIGGER DOLL

King Gobby later step forward, walking a bit closer towards Igworm, smiling, "What are you smiling about?", said Igworm. "Oh, nothing. I was just wondering when you started to play with dolls, that's all", said King Gobby. "I was thinking the same thing", said King Victor. With that everyone behind King Victor laughed. "This doll is a gift from the "Flame of Creation" and what's myself and my new army here to win and NOT you weaklings", said Igworm. King Gobby looked over at King Victor and then back at Igworm, "It is an interesting doll I must say indeed". "It is a Grave Digger doll from the past", said Igworm. "I know, I killed a lot of them in the past, along with my best friend King Josiah", said King Gobby. King Gobby looked over his shoulder and wink at King Victor. King Gobby continued, "The "Flame of Creation" told me something about that doll you have there". "And what is that?", said Igworm. "If you put the Grave Digger doll on the ground, you will have an army of Grave Diggers fighting on your side BUT I find that hard to believe. If that is true, myself, King Victor and the rest of us would not have a prayer in fighting you but I think it is an old-wives-tale", said King Gobby.

Igworm just stared at King Gobby for the moment and later said to him, "Then how come the "Flame of Creation" didn't tell me this information, KING?". "Like you said Igworm, maybe the "Flame of Creation" wants you to win and not us, right? Maybe the "Flame of Creation" already knew that you already now about that special doll. After all, the Grave Diggers DID in fact come from the ground at birth, think about it", said King Gobby, giving a small wink at King Victor again. "Maybe I should lay this doll on the ground and see what happens?", said Igworm.

And with that, the Grave Digger doll went into the ground and up came two hundred and fifty thousand of them. Igworms army had to pull back because of the large number of them. "YOU TRICK ME, THEY ARE ON YOUR SIDE AND NOT MINE. YOU WILL PAY FOR THIS AND I HOPE YOU ARE ALL USED TO A BEATING BECAUSE YOU ARE ABOUT TO GET ONE SO HARD, YOU ARE NOT GOING TO BE ABLE TO THINK TWICE", screamed Igworm.

CHAPTER 49

SPEECH BEFORE THE BATTLE.....AGAIN!

"What can I say Igworm, WE are here to educate you, to help you understand, like don't trust ANYONE", smiled King Victor. "YOU WILL ALL DIE FOR THIS TREACHERY", screamed Igworm again, while everyone was cheering to have the Grave Diggers fight on their side this time (and not fighting them).

"ENOUGH!", shouted Igworm. Everyone at the gates of the Kingdom of Hydra silenced quietly. Igworm stepped forward. A Iggy gave Igworm a sword in one hand and a Wormy gave Igworm a "Katana" in the other hand. Igworm raised the "Katana" in the air and said, "Myself, Iggy's and Wormy's are born here for a reason and that is to rid you pathetic species from this country of Hydra and for that matter of this planet". Everyone of the Iggy's and Wormy's cheered.

King Victor stepped forward, looked over his shoulder at King Gobby, nodded head down and gave him a wink, then back at Igworm. "On my challenge, in ancient laws of combat, we are met on this chosen ground, for good and all, you will be the rulers of Hydra and this planet, us natives, born right wise, while the defiling hoards defiled over it. Also, let the "Flame of Creation" guide my hand against the evil that is in front of us all". Every soldier, village folk, creature, Mermen and Gob-wing cheered so loud, the ground began to shake. "Lets see then if that so-called power of the "Flame of Creation" that just came out of the ground, that so-called Grave Diggers will be any use then", said Igworm. "You will witness the TRUE power of the "Flame of Creation" and teach everyone of you some manners what life is all about", said King Victor. "We will see about that", said Igworm again.

And with that said, both armies clashed with each other and another war will go down in the history books of Hydra......AGAIN.

CHAPTER 50

FULL OUT WAR.....AGAIN!

IGWORMS SIDE

<u>Knights</u>-All the knights look like Wormy. They were all busy taking turns attacking and blocking.

<u>Archers</u>-All the archers look like Wormy. They were busy attacking the Mermen on top of the castle gates and also on the low sides of the mountain range.

<u>Samurai's</u>-And again, all of the samurai's look like Wormy. They were busy fighting alongside the Knights. There speed was something else, a

lot faster then King Victors soldiers, Gob-wings and creatures alike but the Mermen had about the same speed in combat to match-up with the Samurai.

Chemists-All the chemists this time look like Iggy. They were busy healing the rest of the other Iggy's and Wormy's. Also, they did a lot of throwing poison at King Victors men, creatures, Gob-wings and Mermen as well.

Black Mage-All the black mages look like Iggy. They were fantastic when it comes to magic-thunder, fire, ice, water and earth. Especially when it came to long-distance attacks.

White Mage-And again, all of the white mages look like Iggy. They were busy healing all the other Iggy's and Wormy's, making it very difficult for King Victor's soldiers, creatures, Mermen and the Gob-wings alike.

Summoners-The summoners were mixed with Iggy's and Wormy's but they weren't doing anything. They all stayed in the back, patiently waiting for the right time to strike.

<u>KING VICTOR'S SIDE</u>

<u>Knights</u>-Just like the Wormy's, taking turns attacking and blocking.

<u>Archers</u>-The men on the low sides of the mountain range were busy attacking every Iggy and Wormy at random. The same goes for on top of the castle gates.

<u>Village People</u>-They were busy throwing rocks down on top of every Iggy and Wormy close by on top of the castle gates.

<u>Creatures</u>-In the past the creatures used a lot of defense magic but this time, as the years went down the road, they have improved their skills in the offense stage. They cast a lot of magic at the Iggy's and Wormy's like strings of yellow and white mixed.

<u>Mermen</u>-They have improved over the years as well. They are a lot better fighters then five hundred years ago. There speed, strength, stamina and fast thinking killed a lot of Iggy's and Wormy's.

<u>Gob-wings</u>-They were busy fighter the archers, black mages and white mages. The

archers killed quite a few Gob-wings in the process but the Gob-wings killed a lot more white mages and black mages mixed. They even let some archers on King Victor's side to ride them and fire their arrows down at the Iggy's and Wormy's.

<u>Grave Diggers</u>-They were busy just like the knights, fighting the Wormy's off-the knights and samurai's. But later in the fighting, all of the Grave Diggers were making their way to the summoners-mixed Iggy's and Wormy's-because they were to be the strongest of them all. If they were defeated, maybe Igworm would lose confidence in his new breed of minions.

King Victor said to King Gobby, "If we both get close enough, maybe myself and you can throw both of our swords together at Igworm and take him down that way, just like the fake Scarecrow did to King Josiah's father King Luke. I have a weird and strange feeling something might happen if we BOTH do this". "I always said to myself, "Trust your gut", and a lot of times I was right", said King Gobby, with a smirk on his face.

So King Gobby and King Victor started to look for Igworm in the crowd. Finally. Both King Gobby and King Victor saw Igworm. They both fought their way towards him. King Victor shouted at Igworm, saying, "IGWORM, LET'S SEE IF YOU LIKE THIS IN YOUR BELLY- DOUBLE THE FLAVOR".

With that Igworm turned around and before Igworm could make a move, both King Gobby and King Victor threw both of their swords at once and struck Igworm right through the belly, just like King Victor said he was going to do.

But something began to happen to Igworm. He glowed into a dark purple. Very soon after, Igworm lashed out a dark purple beam at both King Gobby and King Victor. All three of them disappeared from the battlefield and later all three fell on the floor in the throne room in King Victor's castle. But their wasn't three of them but FOUR- Iggy and Wormy are back.

As for everyone else outside, they all stopped fighting for the moment. Later they all went back at it again..... fighting, wondering where did Igworm, King Gobby and King Victor went to.

CHAPTER 51

ENCOUNTERING IGGY AND WORMY.....AGAIN!

After a while, King Gobby and King Victor stood up and very surprised to be standing in the throne room. But that wasn't the biggest surprised. Both King Gobby and King Victor saw not one but TWO creatures laying on the floor- it was Iggy and Wormy.

"Just like the fake Scarecrow of the past, when the first "Flame of Creation" was destroyed, he could not pick himself up from the ground because he was in a lot of pain, according to what Queen Sandra said and golly she is right", said King Gobby.

"HA, HA, HA", laughed Iggy. "What us so funny? Both of you have failed, accept your defeat", said King Victor. "You may have defeated us both BUT we have a surprise attack for you and your kind. The summoners are gathering up all their together to summon a powerful beast-which one I truly do not know, HA, HA, HA", laughed Wormy. "Think about it, why do you think ALL of them stayed in the back? So they can gather all their power and not be harmed", said Iggy, with sweat dripping down from his face, with pain, the same goes for Wormy.

King Gobby and King Victor looked at each other. After King Gobby ran towards the window and raised his voice in complete shock, "Iggy and Wormy are right. All of the summoners in the back are collecting all of their power". After King Victor ran towards the window to join King Gobby. Both King Gobby and King Victor saw every summoner cast all their magic into the sky. Then a huge blast of red light, like a big, red cloud, exploded into the sky. With that, every summoner fell to the ground.

"Every summoner fell to the ground, why?", said King Victor. That's because they are all exhausted by collecting ALL the power together as one. The power was too great for them to handle", said King Gobby. "What color is the cloud in the sky the summoners has casted?", said Iggy. "Red", said King Gobby. "They all have summon a beast from the other side and that element is FIRE", said Wormy. "That beast will be here in about five minutes from now and everyone of you will die-humans, creatures, Mermen and those big creatures with wings as well", said Iggy.

King Gobby and King Victor looked at each other, walked away from the window and headed back towards Iggy and Wormy-still laying on the ground in intense pain. "How do we stop this beast from the other side?", said King Victor. "And WHY should we both tell you that?", said Wormy. "If you both want to make a name for yourself FOREVER, now it is the time to do because if that beast kills ALL of us, there will be NO ONE to tell, think about it?", said King Gobby. Both Iggy and Wormy looked over at each other, thinking about what King Gobby have just said. "ALL RIGHT", said Iggy, raising his voice, "You have to kill ONE of us". Wormy spoke right after Iggy, "One of us will get rid of the fire-element-beast and the other will live to tell the story but you MUST kill the right one. We are not allowed to tell you that because there are rules when it comes to the "Flame of Creation", understand?", with lots of sweat dripping from his face, the same for Iggy.

"And what about the other Iggy's and Wormy's?", said King Victor. "They will all be extinct, just like the Grave Diggers of the past and even NOW. They are all connected by the "Flame of Creation", you see", said Iggy. "Makes sense", said King Gobby.

"I think I know which one of the you to kill and bring peace and balance once more and forever for my people and for everyone else for that matter", said King Victor. "Which one?", said King Gobby. "Its Wormy and the reason why I say that is because his symbol is evil-hearted and Iggy's is pure-hearted, think about it, old friend", said King Victor. "True", said King Gobby. So King Victor picked up his sword laying on the floor in the throne room, walked over and looked down on Wormy and said to him, "Rest in peace, Wormy". With that King

Victor drove his sword into Wormy's stomach, bleed out and died. A few seconds later Wormy's body disappeared and the soul of Wormy went into Iggy, Wormy is done for-FOREVER.

As for the red cloud, it disappeared, along with every Iggy and Wormy minion, turning them all into black mud. The same for all the Grave Diggers as well.

CHAPTER 52

VICTORY.....AGAIN!

"Well, I guess it is time to celebrate", said Iggy, as he begin to stand up-free of any kind of pain (with the help of Wormy, of course-soul wise). "HOLD IT", shouted King Victor, "You will be punished for what YOU and WORMY have caused". "I understand", said Iggy.

"Just like five hundred years ago, all of the Grave Diggers including all of the Iggy and Wormy minions turned into black mud", said King Gobby, as he looked out one of the throne room windows. After King Gobby turned around to look at King Victor and said, "Victor,

Iggy should be punished, you are right be WE should give Iggy a second chance to live". "WHAT?", said King Victor, very surprised to hear this coming from King Gobby. "REALLY?", said Iggy, even more surprised then King Victor. "That's right. You helped us Iggy and we are going to help you", said King Gobby, with a smile. "How did Iggy helped us?", said King Victor, very puzzled for the moment.

King Gobby walked over to Iggy and said to him, "When you and Wormy fused together to become Igworm, both of you brought that Grave Digger doll with you. If you didn't show any feeling for it, it would not have worked or for that matter, you would never kept the doll, period. You and Wormy showed love and respect towards the "Flame of Creation", just like all of us. We showed the same thing about this planet, this country and the very people live here around us, think about it. You brought that doll to aid us and didn't realize it. Almost like yourself and Wormy found a way how to convinced the sheep in how to find a way to invite the wolves over for dinner".

"I never thought about it that way", said King Victor. "What will you have me do then", said Iggy, very nervous for the moment. King Gobby patted Iggy on the shoulder and said to him, "You have two choices-one is you will tell this story to EVERYONE about yourself and Wormy helping us with the Grave Diggers OR two-myself and King Victor here will tell everyone your terrible deeds and crimes and you will then be executed. I am fare and so is King Victor. Which one will you choose Iggy?", said King Gobby, with a serious look in his face.

Iggy walked over to one of the throne room windows and looked out. After for a while, Iggy walked back toward to King Gobby and King Victor and said to them both with both hands behind his back, "I will tell everyone about myself and Wormy in helping EVERYONE with the Grave Diggers".

CHAPTER 53

REUNION

"I think that is a beautiful idea", said a strange voice. All three, King Gobby, King Victor and Iggy, turned around very quickly. There they were standing right in front of them, Hope, Queen Sandra and King Scarecrow. "How is this possible?", said King Victor.

Hope walked over to King Gobby, hugged him and said, "All three of us are here for a few minutes only". "We are all so proud of you and we love you so much, "said Queen Sandra. King Scarecrow walked over to Iggy and said, "I get it, the power of the "Flame of Creation" took over you like it did with me, in a way. But I am glad the Grave Diggers were the good guys this time. YOU, IGGY, will have a wonderful and happy life with us human-beings, creatures, Mermen and Gob-wings. I am making you King of the Mermen, my keep is in the mountains and NOW it is yours".

"I have a question for ALL of you, why are you ALL treating me so nice of a sudden?", said Iggy, very confused and at the same time puzzled. "Even enemies can show respect to one another at the end of the day", said Queen Sandra.,while everyone nodding their heads up and down. "That sounds fare", said Iggy, smiling.

"We have to go now brother, our time is over. Again myself, Queen Sandra and King Scarecrow are all proud of you all. Tell everyone what went down here in the throne room. And Iggy don't forget to tell this story to EVERYONE, from the beginning till the end or should I say KING Iggy, "said Hope, smiling. "I will", said Iggy. With that, Hope, Queen Sandra and King Scarecrow went to King Gobby, King Victor and Iggy, one at a time, hugged them and gave them all a kiss. Then they all disappeared one last time and never to appear again.

CHAPTER 54

LEGEND-KING IGGY

"How are you both going to convinced EVERYONE outside of what has happen here inside the castle, here in the throne room?", said Iggy "Actually", said King Victor, as he looked over his shoulder and wink at King Gobby, "YOU, King Iggy, my friend, will tell EVERYONE what really happen in here". "After all, it is your job to tell this story to everyone down the road, right? So it mind as well be doing it NOW,"smiled King Gobby.

"But.....", said King Iggy. "But what?", said King Victor. "But what if they attack me? OR for that matter, KILL me?", said Iggy, very scared for the moment, "I very much doubt it King Iggy and I will tell you why. First off, you are going to tell them all about the Grave Diggers like the doll, yourself and Wormy brought here with you. And when you enter outside the castle doors, everyone will know you are a good creature for two reasons. One is that you will be walking along side myself and King Victor and two, you do not look like Igworm, you look like Iggy. People sometimes judge someone or SOMETHING by their past deeds and looks, trust me, I was there", said King Gobby, looking over at King Victor, raising his eyebrows.

"Plus.....they would NEVER dare harm a living LEGEND. Everyone, including myself and King Gobby here, will see you as a living and breathing "Flame of Creation", if you think about it that way", said King Victor, smiling at King Iggy then back at King Gobby.

"Both of you are right. I will make the human-beings, creatures and the big creatures with wings on their backs listen, understand and respect me. Thank-you King Gobby and King Victor", said King Iggy, as he walked out of the throne room, alongside King Gobby and King Victor.

CHAPTER 55

HISTORY BOOKS OF HYDRA

This is a record kept track by King Iggy of all the events throughout the years in the country of Hydra until he passed away in his keep where the Mermen lived. After his passing, only the generations of priests were allowed to keep record-no one else. The priests were mixed of human-beings, creatures and Mermen, men and women alike. All the records are kept at King Iggy's castle keep. Only anyone with special rights can read them like family members and high priests of each Kingdom. Here is a list of the events of what happen after the victory win over Igworm, kept track by Iggy until he passed away.

<u>King Gobby</u>-King Gobby lived a healthy life, married and has ten children and died of old age - eight hundred years to be exact. He is the very first King of all the creatures and the most respected one of all the creatures. Even now, the creatures celebrate King Gobby for his bravery, hard work and most important his loyalty as being KING. King Woodweed succeeded him as the king of all the creatures, who is King Gobby's first son.

<u>Creatures</u>-They still live in different parts in the country of Hydra-mountains, swamps and even the Kingdom of Hope but some live in the Kingdom of Hydra. Very peaceful with everyone, human-beings and Mermen. The Gob-wings are the same as the creatures BUT they have more pride in themselves because of their wings- the ability to fly. They mostly live in the mountain ranges near King Iggy's castle and other parts in the country as well.

<u>King Victor</u>-King Victor lived a healthy life as well. He took cancer in the blood at age seventy two. He married a beautiful woman

named Faith and has two children, Lewis and Victoria. The same as King Gobby's passing, the people celebrated King Victor (along with many other great kings in their bloodline) every year to honor them of what they have done, His son Lewis got killed from falling off a mountain while hunting. Victoria succeeded King Victor as Queen of Hydra.

<u>King Iggy</u>-King Iggy lived with the Mermen just like King Scarecrow but never married. King Iggy lived a long life like King Gobby, at a good age at seven hundred and fifty five years old. King Iggy was haunted by the memories of his terrible deeds of the past, just like King Scarecrow went through, he could not escape his demons of the past. The only time King Iggy felt relaxed is when King Gobby and King Victor visit him.

<u>Mermen</u>-They kept to themselves a lot because they needed water to live. As the years went by, they would perform private ceremonies in honor of King Iggy and King Scarecrow, each year like everyone else does (but the other ceremonies weren't private) They are more-less loners. Eat, sleep and train is all they know. King Iggy appointed one of

the Mermen to be the head of the castle keep before he passed away.

THE END!